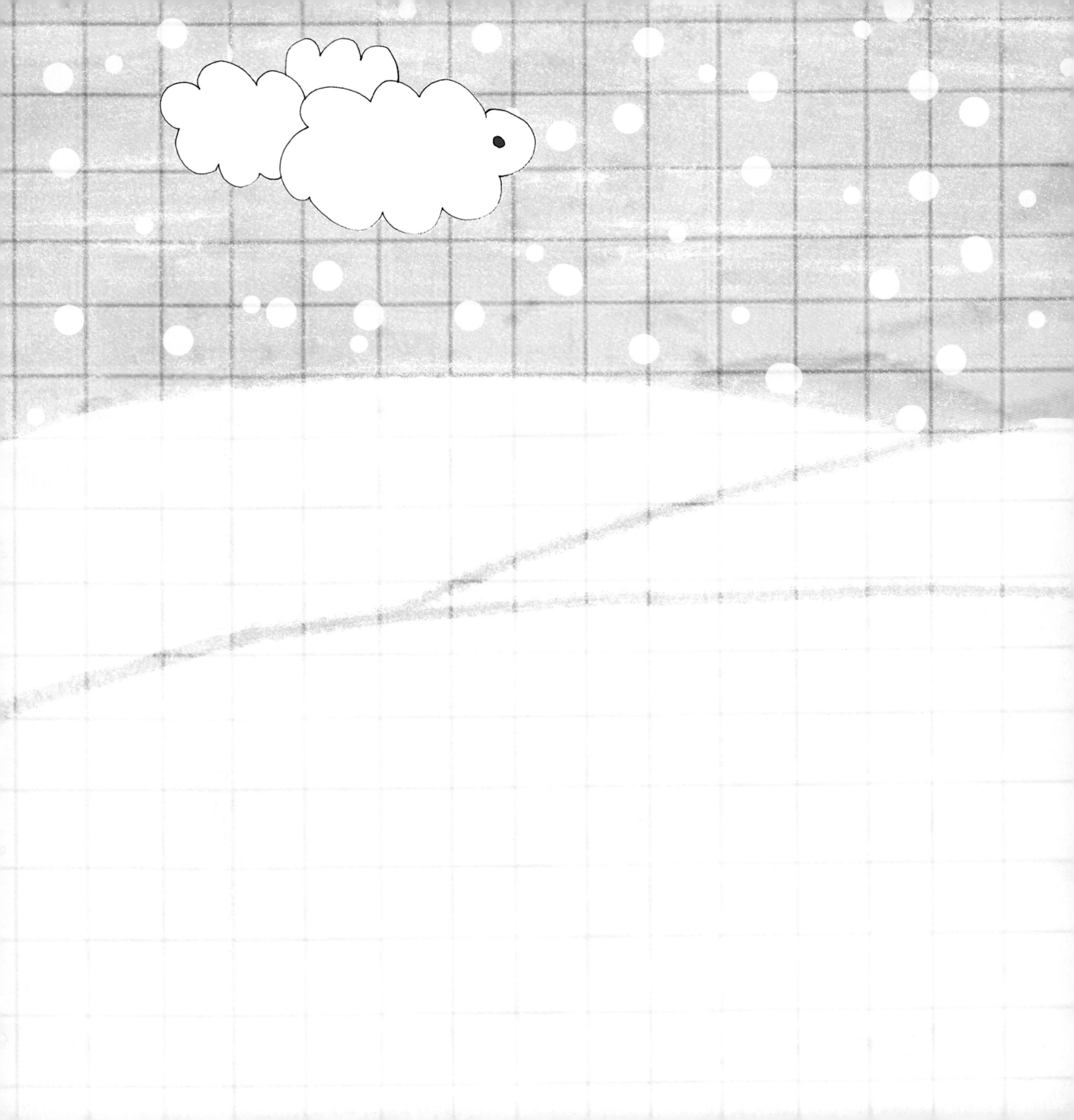

#SnowmanAndTheSun

First published in the UK in 2015 by Tiny Owl Publishing, London
This edition published in the US in 2021 by Tiny Owl Publishing, London
www.tinyowl.co.uk

A CIP record for this book is available from the Library of Congress.

ISBN 978-1-910328-79-8

Printed in China

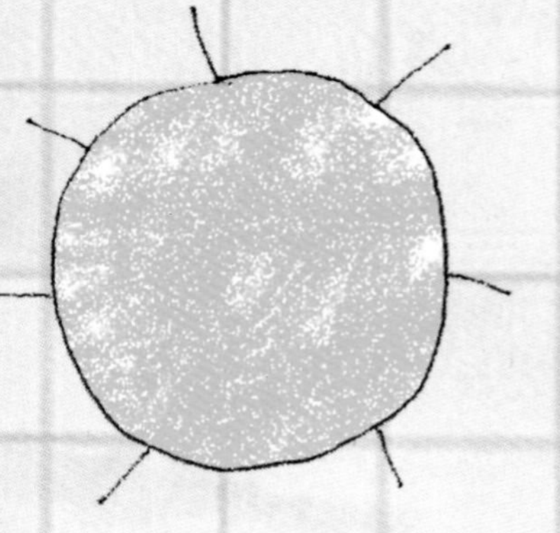

The Snowman and the Sun

Susan Taghdis

Ali Mafakheri

TINY OWL

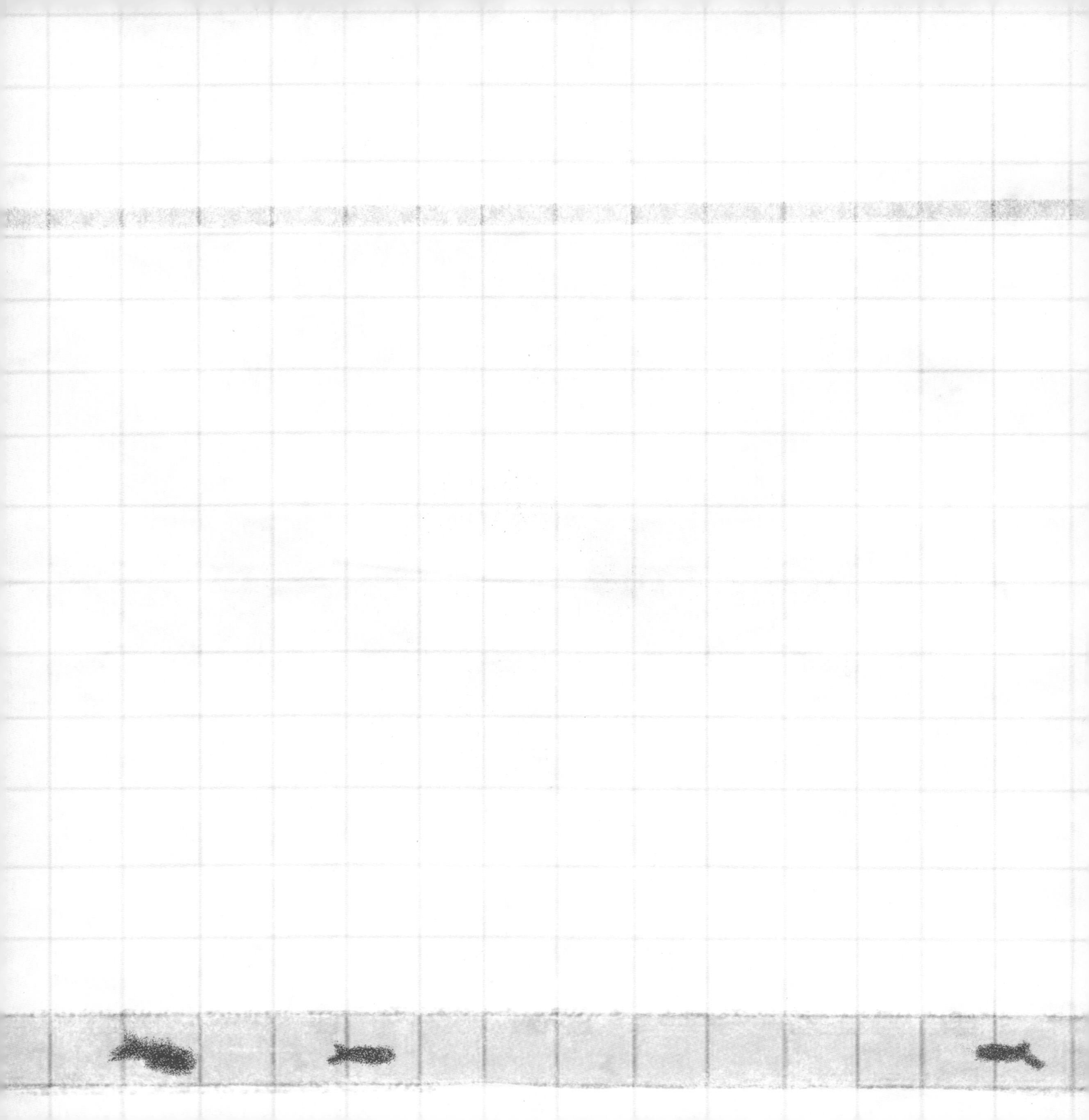

The snowman looked up at the sky.

Way up high, the sun laughed.
"Phew, what a warm sun!" said the snowman. "What happens if I melt?"

The snowman melted and transformed into water.

The snowman ran as
water over the ground.

The ground tickled him. "What warm ground!" said the watery snowman. "I wonder if I will evaporate?"

The snowman changed from water to tiny little water droplets, floating up and up. Then he looked at the sky and said, "Birds are so lucky." Then he kept going up into the cold sky until he became a cloud.

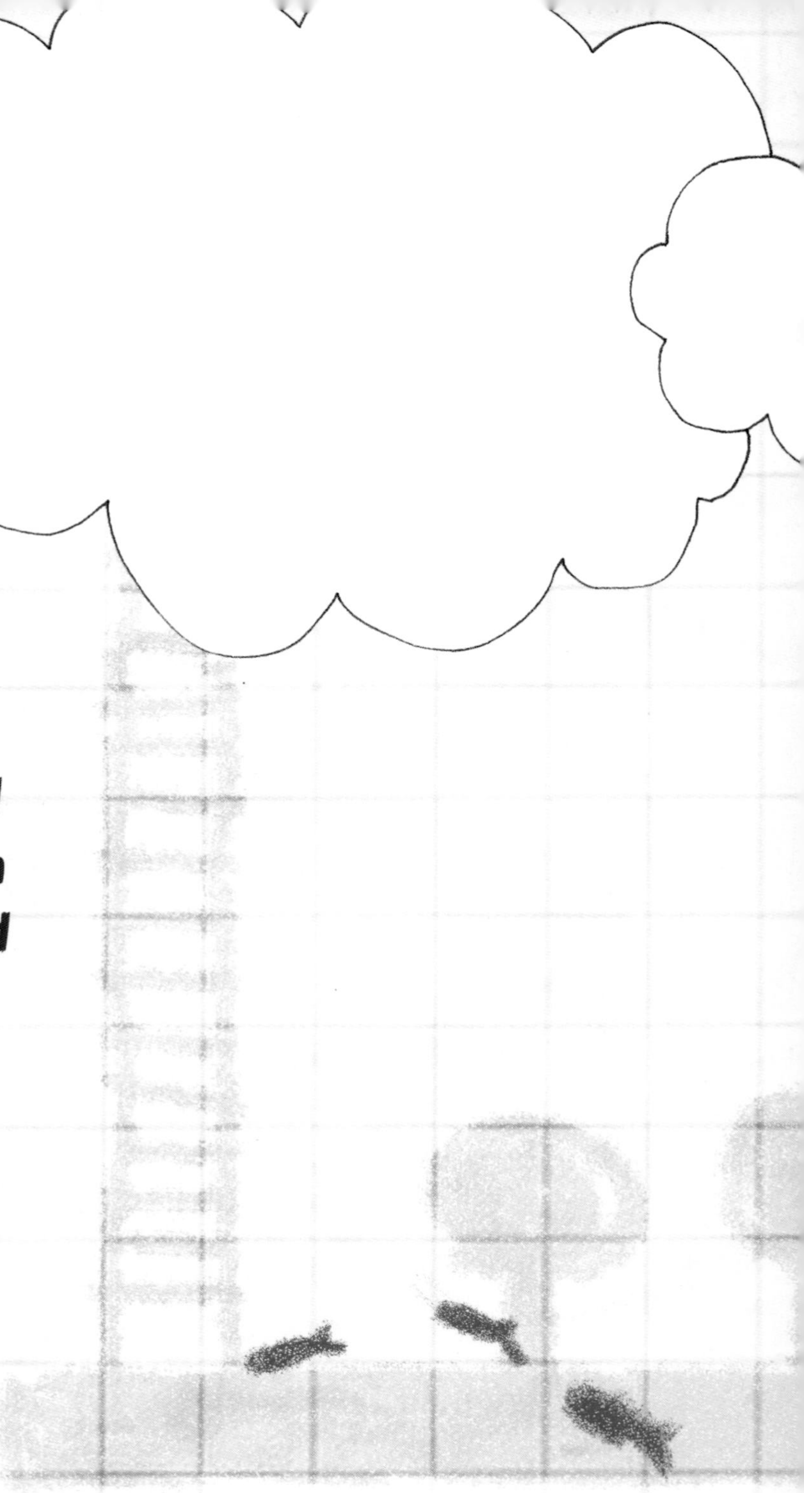

The cloud was free, drifting around in the sky. He went this way and that. "What a nice sky! But what if it gets cold and I turn to snow and fall down?"

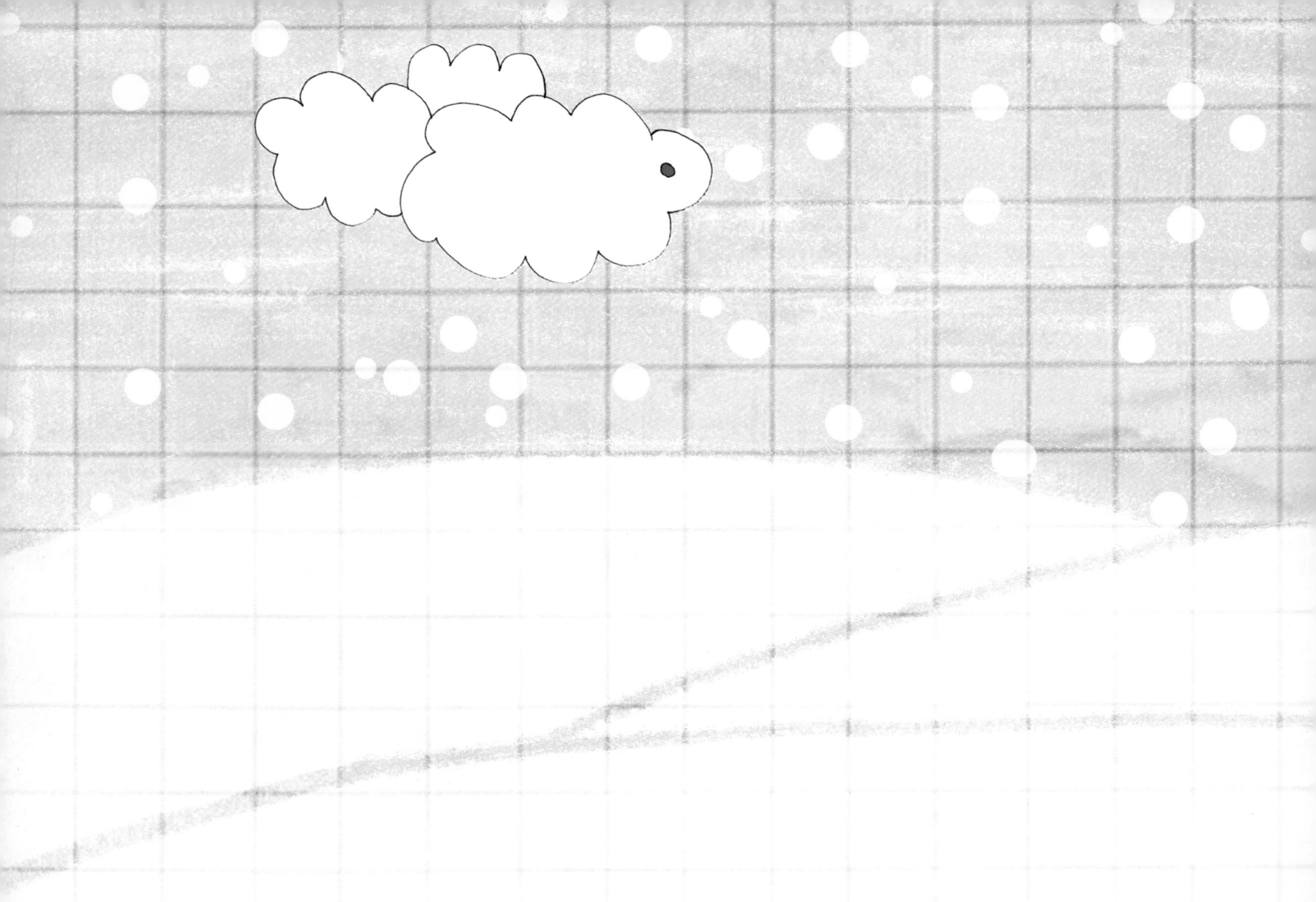

The air then started to get colder. The snowman felt chilly as a cloud. Little by little, he turned back into snow and floated back down to the ground, flake by flake.

The next day when the children woke up, the ground was covered with snow. The snowman, from his big drift of snow, recognized the child looking out of his window.

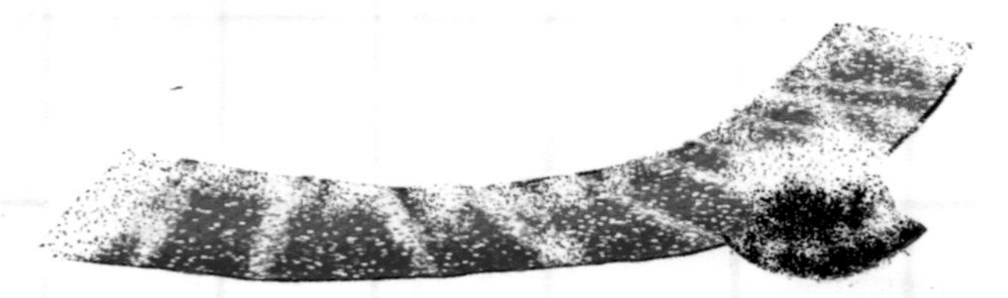

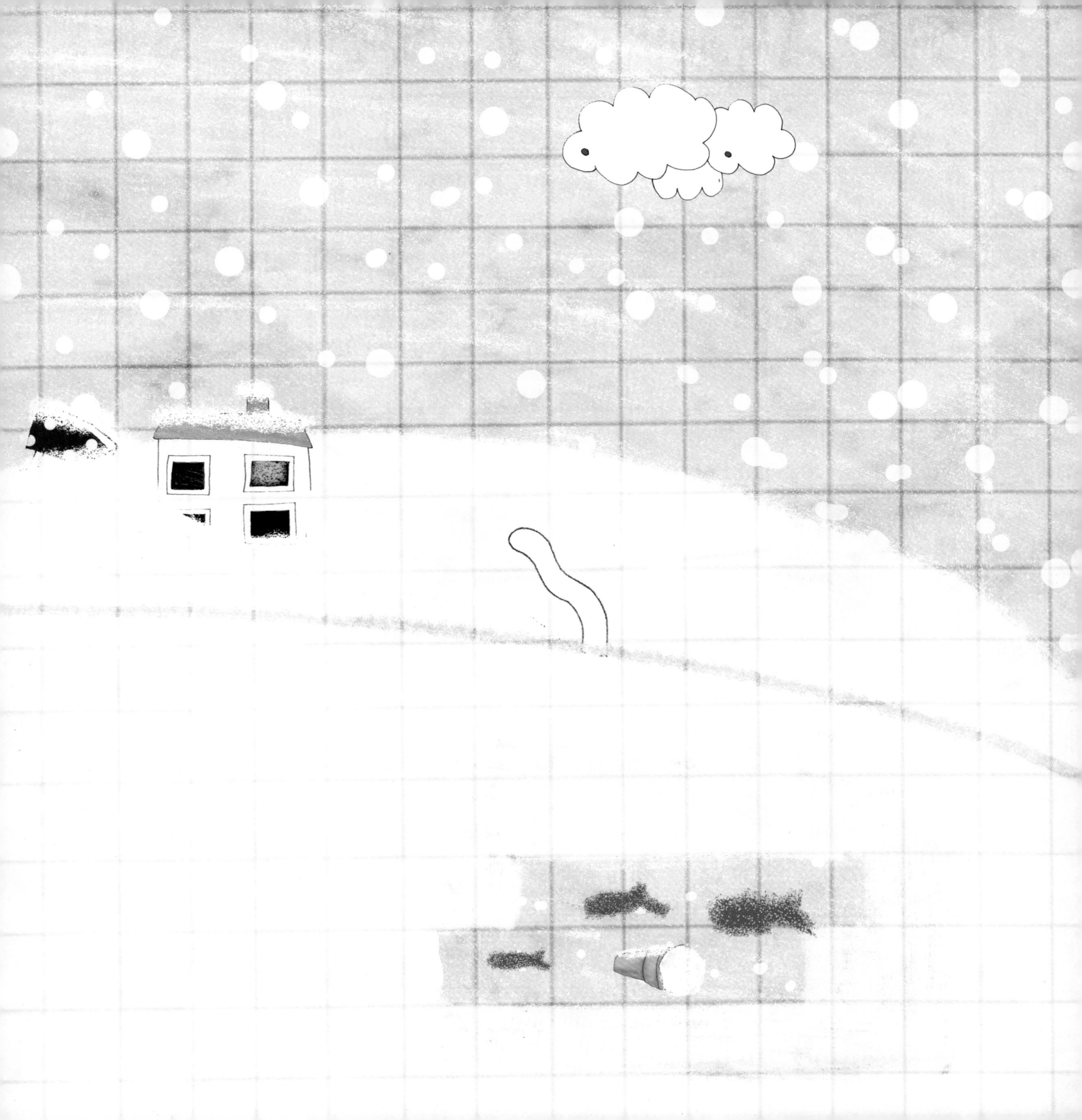

It was the same boy that had turned him into a snowman in the first place. He winked at the boy from the snow and said, "Make a snowman of me!"

Later, the snowman looked up at the sky,
waiting for the sun to appear.

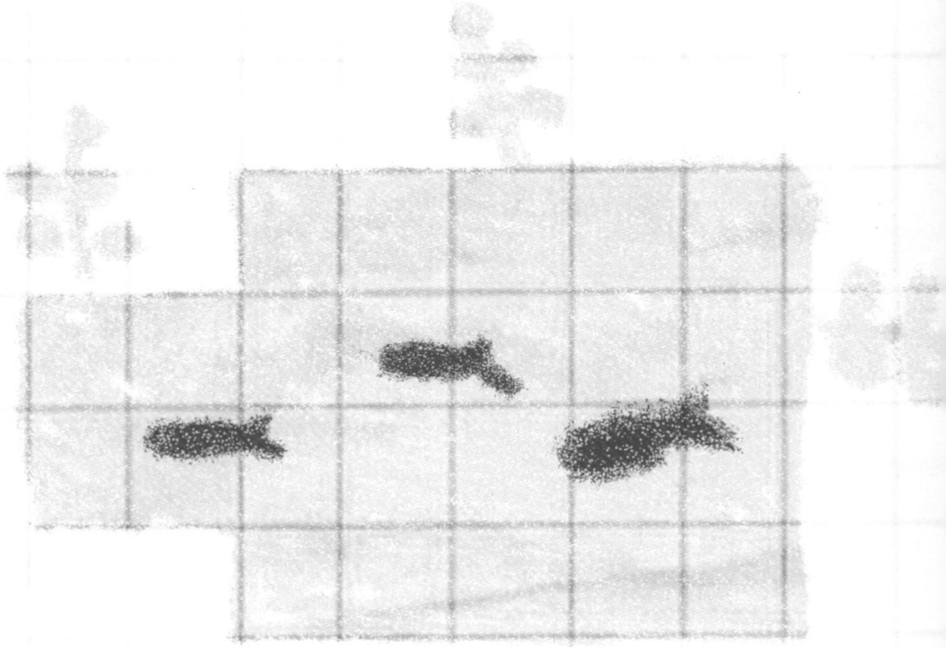

W9-BDP-858

DON'T CALL ME FUZZYBUTT!

BY ROBIN NEWMAN
Illustrated by SUSAN BATORI

Bear needed a lot of sleep. Two hundred and forty-three and a half days, to be precise. Anything less and he turned grizzly.

But Bear had a problem.
He was a very light sleeper.

The slightest noises woke him—falling pine needles,
rustling leaves, a single raindrop.

So he knitted earmuffs and a sleeping cap.

He posted signs everywhere.

And he chopped down trees to make a sturdy front door to keep the noise out of his den.

On hibernation day, Bear took off his bunny slippers,
put on his jammies, and turned out the light.

Before Bear could say "salmon and honey on toasted pumpernickel bread," he was asleep.

Now, Woodpecker was also having a problem. He was a master carpenter, with a specialty in real estate development. He loved building houses.

Every day he pecked holes in his favorite pine trees to make his perfect houses. Twenty pecks per second, to be precise.

But lately his houses were disappearing.

"WHAT HAPPENED TO MY RUSTIC RANCH, COZY COTTAGE, AND SOLAR-POWERED DUPLEX?"

Woodpecker went looking.

He asked Rabbit, who talked to Mouse, who called Squirrel.
No one had seen a thing.

He posted flyers around the neighborhood and even offered a reward.

One morning, Woodpecker noticed something on the ground.

"Is that my door?"

Woodpecker took a closer look.

"Wait a second! And that's part of my roof!"

Woodpecker kept his eyes glued to the ground. There, he found bits and pieces from each of the perfectly pecked houses he had built. And these bits and pieces became a trail that led him straight to Bear's new front door.

"My houses!" exclaimed Woodpecker.

But all of his houses were destroyed.

So Woodpecker went straight to work.

PECK!

"Quiet," Bear grumbled.

PECK!
PECK!

Bear pulled the covers tight and started counting buzzing bees.

PECK!
PECK!
PECK!

And

PECK!

home
SWEET in

That last **PECK** was the last straw.

Bear's fur bristled, his brows twitched, his nostrils flared, and from his very big mouth with very sharp teeth (42, to be precise!), he roared a mighty

ROAR.

"WHO'S THE PESKY **FEATHERBUTT**
MAKING THAT NOISE?"

Rabbit, Mouse, and Squirrel could not believe their ears.

"Bear called Woodpecker a featherbutt!" Rabbit gabbed to Mouse, who then blabbed to Squirrel.

"Excuse me. Did you call me a pesky weatherbutt?" asked Woodpecker, flying right up to Bear. "That wasn't nice."

"No, I called you a pesky featherbutt. **GOOD NIGHT!**"

Bear crawled back into bed, tossed the pillow over his head,
switched off the lamp, and quickly fell back asleep, when . . .

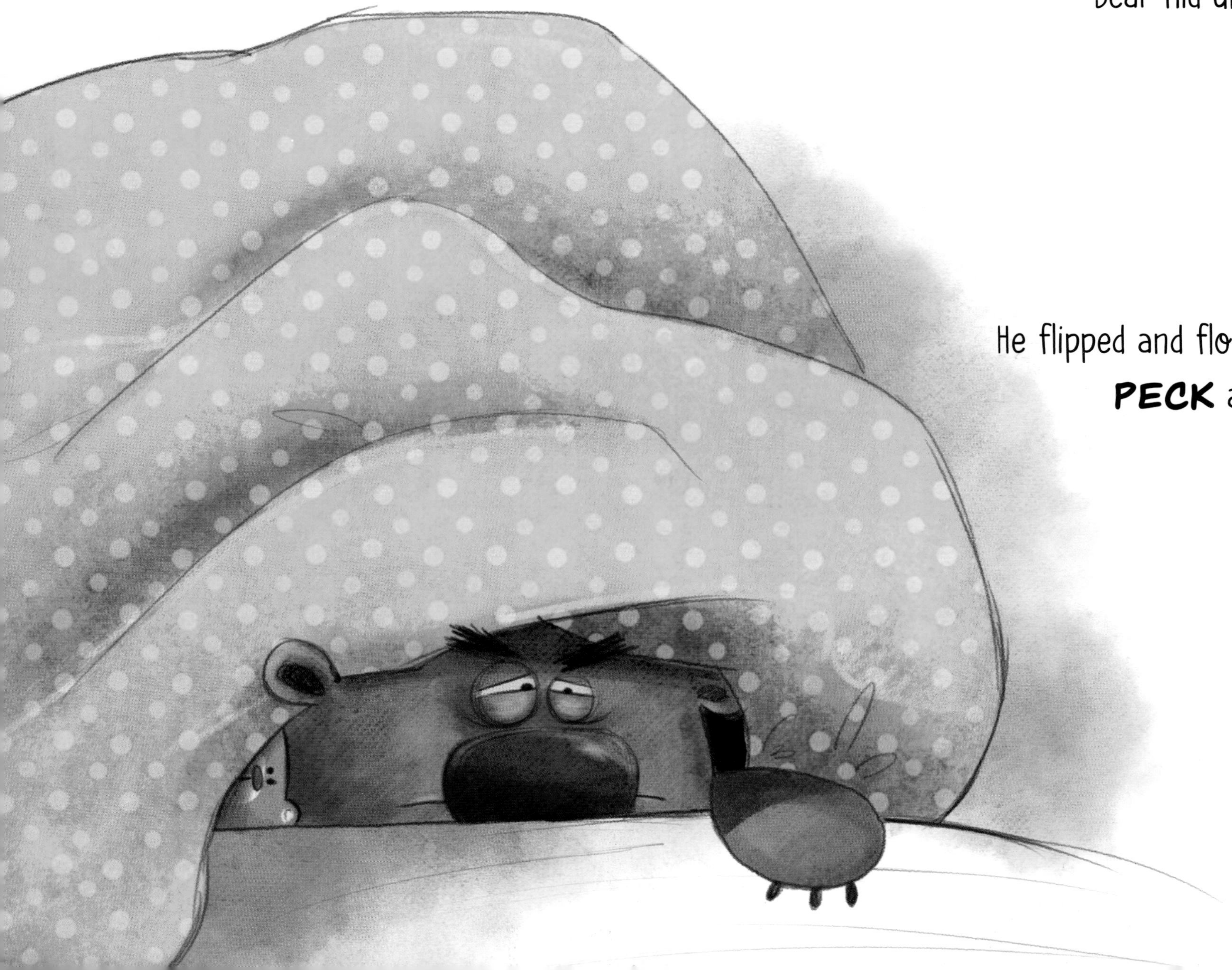

PECK!
SNIFFLE.

Bear hid under the covers.

PECK!
PECK!
SNIFFLE.

He flipped and flopped with every
PECK and **SNIFFLE**.

Bear switched on his lamp, grabbed a tissue, and opened the door.

"Here," said Bear. "Blow your nose, stop pecking, and stop crying."

"You called me a pesky featherbutt . . .
in front of everyone!"

"I'm sorry but if I don't get my sleep, I become

A GREAT . . .

SNARL . . .

BIG . . .

GROWL . . .

GRIZZLY . . .

ROAR . . .

BEAR!"

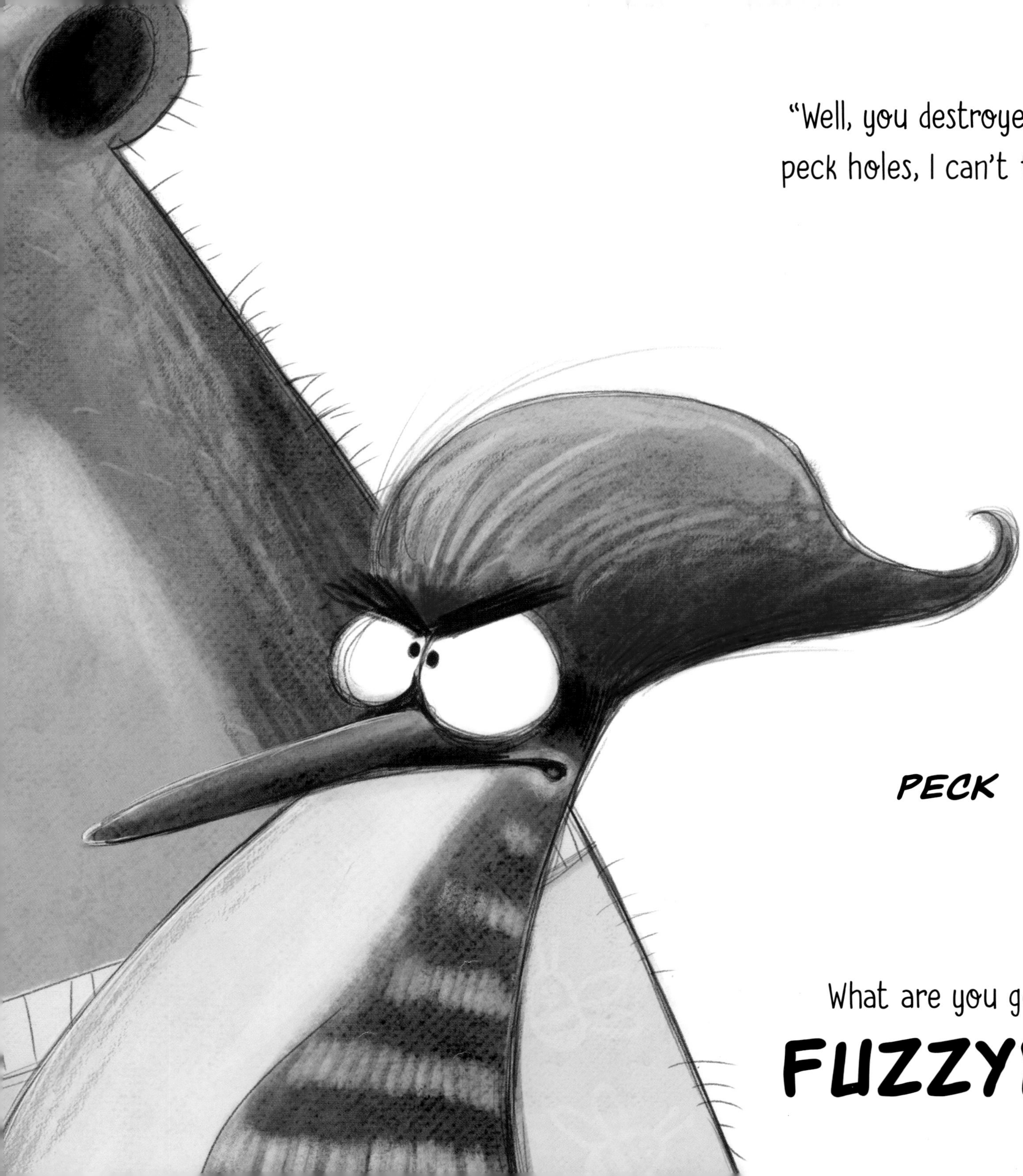

"Well, you destroyed my houses. If I don't peck holes, I can't fix them and I become

A VERY . . .

PECK . . .

ANNOYING . . .

PECK . . .

GROUCHY . . .

PECK PECK PECK

PEST!

What are you going to do about that,

FUZZYBUTT?"

Rabbit, Mouse, and Squirrel could not believe their ears.

"Woodpecker called Bear a fuzzybutt!"

Rabbit gabbed to Mouse, who confided in Squirrel, who then blabbed to Bear.

"I'm right here! I heard what he said."

Bear **STOMPED**.

He **ROARED**.

And he slammed the door shut!

"GOOD NIGHT, AGAIN!"

Nobody had ever called him a fuzzybutt.

He crawled back to bed and turned out the light.

"I'm not a fuzzybutt!" Bear whispered to his teddy bear.

In the darkness, there was the sound of a faint sniffle.

Woodpecker quietly opened the door and flew into Bear's den.
Then he switched on the lamp and handed Bear a tissue.

“I’m sorry, Bear. I didn’t mean to call you a fuzzybutt.”

“I’m sorry, too! I didn’t mean to call you a weatherbutt . . . I mean featherbutt . . . I mean . . .”

“Apology accepted,” said Woodpecker.

So Bear and Woodpecker put their heads together and came up with a plan. Woodpecker pecked while Bear hammered and sawed.

They repaired Woodpecker's houses and moved them far, far away from Bear's den.

They also made Bear a brand-new door.

Then Woodpecker tucked Bear into bed. "See you in the spring!"

Before Bear could say "salmon and honey on toasted pumpernickel bread," he was sound asleep.

SHHH

Bear slept two hundred and forty-three and a half days . . .

while Woodpecker pecked his holes—
twenty pecks per second, to be precise.

When Bear woke in the spring, Woodpecker could hardly wait to ask him something.

"What's a featherbutt?"

"I don't know. What's a fuzzybutt?"

"Beats me."

With love for my favorite fuzzybutts, Michael and Noah

Heartfelt thanks to Sarah Rockett, Liza Fleissig, Ginger Harris-Dontzin, and to the Bank Street Writers lab for their endless encouragement and support

—RN

♥

To Robert, who is my giant, loveable Teddy Bear

—SB

SLEEPING BEAR PRESS™
2395 South Huron Parkway, Suite 200
Ann Arbor, MI 48104
www.sleepingbearpress.com

Printed and bound in the United States.

10 9 8 7 6 5 4 3 2 1

Library of Congress Cataloging-in-Publication Data

Names: Newman, Robin, author. | Batori, Susan, illustrator.
Title: Don't call me fuzzybutt! / by Robin Newman ; illustrated by Susan Batori.
Other titles: Do not call me fuzzybutt!
Description: Ann Arbor, Michigan : Sleeping Bear Press, [2021] |
Audience: Ages 6-10. | Summary: As Bear settles into his bed for hibernation Woodpecker, shocked to discover his cherished homes are missing, follows the trail of debris right to Bear's new front door, where a feisty exchange of name-calling and neighborhood gossip ensues.
Identifiers: LCCN 2020039806 | ISBN 9781534110731 (hardcover)
Subjects: CYAC: Bears–Fiction. | Woodpeckers–Fiction. | Interpersonal relations–Fiction.
Classification: LCC PZ7.1.N486 Do 2021 | DDC [E]–dc23
LC record available at https://lccn.loc.gov/2020039806